Robert Quackenbush

Bicycle to Treachery

A Miss Mallard Mystery

·

Simon & Schuster Books for Young Readers

Published by Simon & Schuster

New York   London   Toronto   Sydney   Tokyo   Singapore

SIMON & SCHUSTER
BOOKS FOR YOUNG READERS
Simon & Schuster Building, Rockefeller Center
1230 Avenue of the Americas, New York, New York 10020

SIMON & SCHUSTER BOOKS FOR YOUNG READERS
is a trademark of Simon & Schuster

Manufactured in the United States of America
Also available in a hardcover edition.

10 9 8 7 6 5 4 3 2 1

Library of Congress Cataloging-in-Publication Data

Quackenbush, Robert M.
  Bicycle to treachery.

  Summary: While on a bicycle trip across Holland,
Miss Mallard runs into danger when she unwittingly
uncovers a smuggling operation.
  [1. Mystery and detective stories.   2. Ducks—
Fiction]   I. Title.
PZ7.Q16Bi 1985   [Fic]   85-9483
  ISBN 0-13-076258-X
  ISBN 0-671-73346-X (pbk)

For Piet and Margie

While on a bicycle tour of Holland, Miss Mallard—the world-famous ducktective— took a wrong turn. She became separated from the other cyclists. When she got back on the right road, the tour group was nowhere in sight.

All day Miss Mallard pedaled hard and fast to catch up, but she was still too far behind. And she was so tired and hungry! Finally she decided to look for a place where she could have supper and spend the night. Soon she came to an inn.

Miss Mallard parked her bicycle and entered the inn. The inside was very gloomy, with dark woodwork and furniture. Everything lacked color. Even the flower vases were empty.

"Oh, well," thought Miss Mallard. "It will do for one night."

She signed her name in the guestbook.

"I'll pay for the room now," she said to the innkeeper. "I'll be leaving quite early in the morning. I'm hoping to catch up with my tour."

"Your room is the first door to the left as you go upstairs," said the innkeeper as he handed her a key. "Supper is now being served in the dining room."

Miss Mallard went up to her room to unpack her knitting bag. Then she went to the dining room. There she met another guest at the inn, Julia Pintail, who invited Miss Mallard to sit at her table.

"I'm so glad to meet you, Miss Mallard," said Julia. "Your name is known all over the world."

During supper the two of them chatted about their travels. But all the while Miss Mallard noticed that her dinner companion was very nervous. Julia kept glancing at the dining room entrance. From time to time she took a small black book from her purse and scribbled a few words in it.

Suddenly, while they were having dessert, two tough-looking ducks appeared at the dining room entrance. In a flash, Julia ducked under the table.

"Pretend I'm not here," she whispered to Miss Mallard. "Tell me when those two ducks leave."

Miss Mallard waited. She saw the two ducks look around the room. Then they vanished.

"It's safe now," said Miss Mallard to Julia. "They're gone."

Julia came out from under the table and said, "Do you think they saw me?"

"I can't be certain," said Miss Mallard. "What is this about?"

"I can tell you because I trust you," said Julia. "But you must tell no one else. I am a secret agent. In a bookshop in Amsterdam, I accidentally learned that a ring of smugglers has its headquarters in this area. They are smuggling stolen diamonds, china, and old-master paintings out of the country. I'm positive that those two ducks are part of the ring. They have been following me everywhere. They are henchducks."

"Dear me!" said Miss Mallard. "Can't you notify the police?"

"Not until I find the mastermind of the operation," said Julia. "Then I plan to go to the police."

"Can I help?" asked Miss Mallard.

"In a way you are helping right now," said Julia. "I'll tell you about it in the morning. Please knock on my door when you are ready to leave. I'm in room three."

"Is six o'clock too early for you?" asked Miss Mallard.

"The earlier the better," replied Julia.

With that, they both said "goodnight" and went to their rooms.

Promptly at six the next morning, Miss Mallard knocked on Julia's door. There was no answer. Miss Mallard knocked again. Still there was no answer. She turned the doorknob and the door opened. She peeked inside the room. Julia was gone and so were her things!

Miss Mallard ran to the lobby to ask the innkeeper if he had seen Julia.

"Miss Pintail checked out late last night," said the innkeeper. "Two friends came for her."

"Friends?" asked Miss Mallard. "Were they wearing trench coats and dark glasses?"

"I don't know," answered the innkeeper. "I wasn't here at the time."

Miss Mallard shivered. She was sure
that Julia had been ducknapped. She fled
from the lobby and hurried up the stairs.

Back in her room, she reached for her
knitting bag on the bed. She felt around
inside the bag to see if she had packed
everything. She touched something
unfamiliar and pulled it out of the bag.

"Julia's black book!" Miss Mallard
gasped.

Suddenly, everything was clear to Miss Mallard. At supper, Julia had slipped the black book into Miss Mallard's knitting bag for safekeeping. She planned to ask for it when Miss Mallard knocked on her door the following morning.

Miss Mallard thumbed through the black book. Julia's last entry was written in code:

REVOY EHTM EGDIRBO
EHTZ SDOOGR ERAT DEROTSN;
DNIFC EHTY REZEENST,
EHW SDNIMRETSAMP EHTQ DRAOHV!

"There's no time to decode this," thought Miss Mallard. "I must go to the police at once."

She went to the window to see if it was safe to leave. The two henchducks were waiting outside!

"Oh, dear," thought Miss Mallard. "The henchducks must have seen Julia and me together at dinner after all. They've figured out that she gave the black book to me. But what have they done with her? What will they do to me?"

Miss Mallard wondered how she could get past the henchducks. Then she remembered a Dutch costume, complete with wooden shoes, that she had bought during her travels. She pulled it out of her knitting bag. Quickly, she changed into the costume. Then she ran down the back stairs of the inn.

Outside, Miss Mallard saw a pail and a broom by the back door. She put her knitting bag in the pail and took the pail and broom to the front of the inn. Then she began sweeping the front walk as though she was a maid for the inn. Fooled by her disguise, the henchducks paid no attention to her.

As Miss Mallard swept, she kept edging closer to her bicycle, which was behind a tree. When she was close enough, she hopped onto it and took off. But it was hard to pedal in wooden shoes. They fell off her feet and hit the ground with a clatter. Snatching them up, Miss Mallard tossed them into her knitting bag and hurried on.

Miss Mallard pedaled with all her might
across a field behind the inn. Then she saw
a speeding car racing along the road. One
of the henchducks was inside!

"Oh, no!" cried Miss Mallard aloud.
"They saw me escape!"

There was no turning back. There was
no going forward. A henchduck awaited her
at each end of the field. What could she do?

She got off her bicycle and stood frozen
in her tracks.

Just then, a tractor came racing out from a cluster of trees. It stopped in front of Miss Mallard.

"What are you doing in my field?" demanded the farmer who was driving the tractor.

Before Miss Mallard could answer, he climbed down from his tractor, tossed Miss Mallard's bicycle on the back, and helped her aboard. Then he sped back to the group of trees.

"I'm sorry if I disturbed your field," said Miss Mallard as she climbed down from the tractor.

The farmer sneezed loudly.

"Blasted cold!" he said as he set Miss Mallard's bicycle on the ground.

"Here," said Miss Mallard. "Take one of my hankies. I'll be on my way."

She hopped on her bicycle and left the still sneezing farmer. She pedaled quickly onto a path. She knew that the henchducks would soon be after her. She had to find a place to hide. She raced along the path until she came to a bridge that led to a windmill.

"The only place!" said Miss Mallard.

She got off her bicycle and hauled it under the bridge.

Safely hidden under the bridge, Miss
Mallard set to work to decode the last
entry in Julia's black book. She discovered
that the words were written backwards,
with an extra letter added at the end of
each word. The decoded message said:

OVER THE BRIDGE
THE GOODS ARE STORED;
FIND THE SNEEZER,
HE MASTERMINDS THE HOARD!

"Good grief!" thought Miss Mallard.
"This tells where the smugglers hide their
loot. But does it mean over *this* bridge?
And who is The Sneezer?"

At that moment, Miss Mallard heard footsteps. The henchducks were standing overhead on the bridge!

"Did you check the windmill?" asked the first henchduck.

"She wasn't there," said the second henchduck. "What if we can't find her?"

"You know The Sneezer's orders," came the answer. "He wants that book! If we can't find her, we are to open the flood gates of the dike to keep our operation from being discovered. So let's go back to the car and keep looking. She couldn't have gotten far on a bicycle."

Miss Mallard kept very quiet until she heard a car drive away. Then she grabbed her bicycle and carried it up to the path. She looked all around. The henchducks were nowhere in sight. She looked at the windmill beyond the bridge and remembered Julia's secret message in the black book.

"Let me see," thought Miss Mallard. "Julia said, 'Over the bridge the goods are stored.' That's it! The smuggled goods are in the windmill."

She went to the windmill and peeked through a window. Sure enough, the inside was filled with boxes and crates of stolen goods. Then she tried the door. The henchducks had forgotten to lock it!

Miss Mallard ran inside the windmill and up the winding stairs to the top. She looked out a small window. Down below she could see the inn, and the innkeeper standing at the back door. Nearby was the field that she had crossed, the cluster of trees, and the farmer repairing his tractor. Beside the field was a winding road and the henchducks' speeding car. At the end of the road was a tiny town.

Miss Mallard narrowed her eyes. She could see a police station in the town. Policeducks were standing in front of the station. She got an idea.

"I hope my plan works," she said.

Quickly, Miss Mallard took a mirror from her knitting bag. Holding it so it caught the sun, she began signaling the police station. Her message in Morse code was three short flashes, three long flashes, and three more short flashes: S-O-S.

Suddenly, one of the policeducks saw the signal and pointed it out to the others. They all got on bicycles and began racing toward the windmill.

Miss Mallard kept on signaling. The henchducks, the innkeeper, and the farmer saw the signals. They came running toward Miss Mallard, too.

The henchducks, the innkeeper, and the farmer got to the windmill before the police. Miss Mallard heard the door open below and footsteps racing up the stairs. They were getting closer and closer.

Miss Mallard waited for the right moment. Then, holding her knitting bag, she leaped from the window. With her free wing, she grabbed a sail of the windmill and rode swiftly to the ground. Letting go of the sail, she took hold of a rope and tied it to the wall. This made the sails stop turning, with one blocking the tiny window. Then Miss Mallard shoved a stick through the handles of the door.

"There," said Miss Mallard. "That should keep everyone locked up until the police get here."

When the police arrived, Miss Mallard told them about Julia, the black book, and the smuggling ring.

"The leader of the ring—The Sneezer—is inside the windmill," said Miss Mallard.

She removed the stick that fastened the door. Out came the two henchducks, the farmer, and the innkeeper. The farmer sneezed loudly, "AAACHOO!" The policeducks grabbed him.

"Not him," said Miss Mallard. "He's not The Sneezer, he only has a cold. He probably came here out of curiosity."

She took a bottle from her knitting bag and started to spray perfume into the air.

"No! No! Stop!" yelled the innkeeper.
"I'm allergic!"

Miss Mallard turned to the policeducks.

"There is your confession," she said. "The
Sneezer is the innkeeper. The inn is his
hideout and his hoard is in the windmill.
These are his henchducks. He is allergic to
flowers and perfume. I knew that when I
saw the empty vases in the inn. I suspected
him when he said *two* friends came for
Julia. How could he have known that, when
he claimed he was not there at the time?"

"What have you done with Julia?" the
police chief asked the innkeeper.

"She's back at the inn," grumbled the
innkeeper. "I locked her in the attic."

"I'll go rescue her," said one of the policeducks.

The chief of police turned to Miss Mallard and said, "How can we ever thank you?"

"Easy," answered Miss Mallard. "Show me the quickest way back to my tour. They are a hearty group of cyclists and I'm anxious to rejoin them."

"Consider it done," said the chief. "I'll escort you there myself."

"What a thrill!" exclaimed Miss Mallard.

48